My Sound Box

by Jane Belk Moncure

illustrated by Vera Gohman

THE CHILD'S WORLD

MANKATO, MN 56001

Library of Congress Cataloging in Publication Data

Moncure, Jane Belk.
  My "i" sound box.

  (Sound box books)
  Summary: Little i finds many things beginning with
the letter i to put in her sound box.
    1. Children's stories, American.   [1. Alphabet]
I. Gohman, Vera Kennedy, 1922-   ill. II. Title.
III. Series.
PZ7.M739Myi 1984   [E]   84-17022
ISBN 0-89565-298-6 -1991 Edition

My "i" Sound Box

(This book concentrates on the short "i" sound in the story line. Words beginning with the long "i" sound are included at the end of the book.)

Little  had a box.

"I will find things that begin with
my 'i' sound," she said.

"I will put them
into my sound  box."

Little went skip, skip,
skip up a hill.

She found inchworms,

lots of little
inchworms.

The inchworms wiggled
and wiggled.

"What wiggly
inchworms," she said.

Did she put the inchworms
into her box?

She did.

Then Little

found

iguanas,

lots of iguanas.

11

The iguanas wiggled
and wiggled.

"What wiggly iguanas," she said.

She put the iguanas

into the box with the inchworms.

But the inchworms did not like the iguanas!

The inchworms jumped
out of the box.

The iguanas jumped out too.

Away they went!

Little could not find the inchworms or

the
iguanas.

They were hiding.

17

Then Little

found an igloo.

Did she put the igloo into her box?

She did.

Just then, the sun came out.

Guess what?

The igloo melted away.

"Now, who will help me
fill my box?" she said.

An Indian came by.

"I will help you
       fill your box," she said.

The Indian found

an Indian dress,

Indian moccasins,

Indian beads,

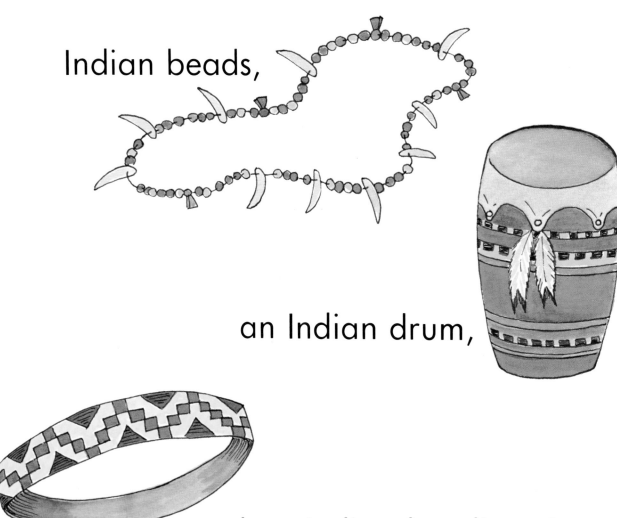

an Indian drum,

and an Indian headband.

Guess where they put the Indian things?
Now the box was full.

"Thank you," said Little .

"Now I will dress like an Indian."

And she did!

inchworms

Indian

iguana

Can you read these words with Little ?

insect

ink

infant

imp

inch

inn

Little  has another sound in some words. She says her name, "i."

Can you read these words?
Listen for Little 's name.

ice cubes

ice cream

icicle

island

ivy

iceberg

About the Author

Jane Belk Moncure began her writing career when she was in kindergarten. She has never stopped writing. Many of her children's stories and poems have been published, to the delight of young readers, including her son Jim, whose childhood experiences found their way into many of her books.

Mrs. Moncure's writing is based upon an active career in early childhood education. A recipient of an M.A. degree from Columbia University, Mrs. Moncure has taught and directed nursery, kindergarten, and primary grade programs in California, New York, Virginia, and North Carolina. As a member of the faculties of Virginia Commonwealth University and the University of Richmond, she taught prospective teachers in early childhood education.

Mrs. Moncure has traveled extensively abroad, studying early childhood programs in the United Kingdom, The Netherlands, and Switzerland. She was the first president of the Virginia Association for Early Childhood Education and received its award for oustanding service to young children.

A resident of North Carolina, Mrs. Moncure is currently a full-time writer and educational consultant. She is married to Dr. James A. Moncure, former vice president of Elon College.